For: _____

With love: _____

Dream

with Sesame Street

Words by Susanna Leonard Hill
Pictures by Marybeth Nelson

A dream can be big or a dream can be small.

What matters the most is to have dreams at all.

Ambitious, creative, outrageous, concrete,

or close to your heart, something simple and sweet.

A dream can be near or a dream can be far.

It even can push you to reach for the stars.

Wherever you go, way up to new heights,

if you keep trying, your dreams will take flight!

Though beginning seems hard with no ending in sight,

each story begins with the first word you write.

A single note starts the most beautiful song.

One step gets your dream up and moving along.

When things don't work out in just the right ways,

remember you grow when you get through bad days.

Don't be scared of a monster hiding on the next page.

Keep learning, keep dreaming, no matter your age!

Since one person's trash is another one's treasure,

your dreams are not subject to anyone's measure.

Even if others may not think it's best,

the road to success is your own special quest.

It's perfectly fine to do things your own way.

However you do them, it's always okay.

How boring if everyone did things the same.

So imagine! Have fun! And play your own game!

Sometimes big ideas don't go as you planned.

Giant leaps lead to stumbles and falls when you land.

But pick yourself up. Try again the next day.

Get back on that stage—everything's A-OK!

A wand isn't needed to make dreams come true.

The magic you need is already in you!

Forget about fairy dust, potions, and spells.

You've got all you need to succeed and excel!

If your dream is too big to complete on your own,

teamwork is better than working alone.

You always can ask a good friend for advice,

and working together sure does feel nice!

If you're worried about making a lot of mistakes,

and wondering whether you have what it takes,

remember you don't need a superhero's cape!

Just believe in yourself and your dreams will take shape.

Though you're sure to have days when you can't try a smile,

look on the sweet side of life for a while.

Cookies and milk sweep the gray clouds away

and bring you right back to a bright sunny day.

Some dreams you will hold very close to your heart

but others are better when friends can take part.

If your dream seems as if it will never come true,

keep in mind you're surrounded by those who love you.

You're amazing and smart in all that you do.

Count your blessings for all that is given to you.

Make every day count to achieve something new.

Every day is a chance for a dream to come true.

Although you work hard toward your dreams every day,

make sure you take time out to giggle and play.

Be happy. Be silly. Make a funny face!

Reaching your dreams is not some big race.

When one dream is realized, the next can shine through,

pushing you forward to try something new.

Never stop dreaming, whatever you do.

Here's wishing that all of your dreams will come true!

Cover and internal design © 2019 by Sourcebooks
Text by Susanna Leonard Hill
Illustrations by Marybeth Nelson

Sourcebooks and the colophon are registered trademarks of Sourcebooks, Inc.

Published by Sourcebooks Wonderland, an imprint of Sourcebooks Kids
P.O. Box 4410, Naperville, Illinois 60567-4410
(630) 961-3900
sourcebookskids.com

Source of Production: 1010 Printing Asia Limited, North Point, Hong Kong, China
Date of Production: July 2019
Run Number: 5015738

Printed and bound in China.
OGP 10 9 8 7 6 5 4 3 2 1